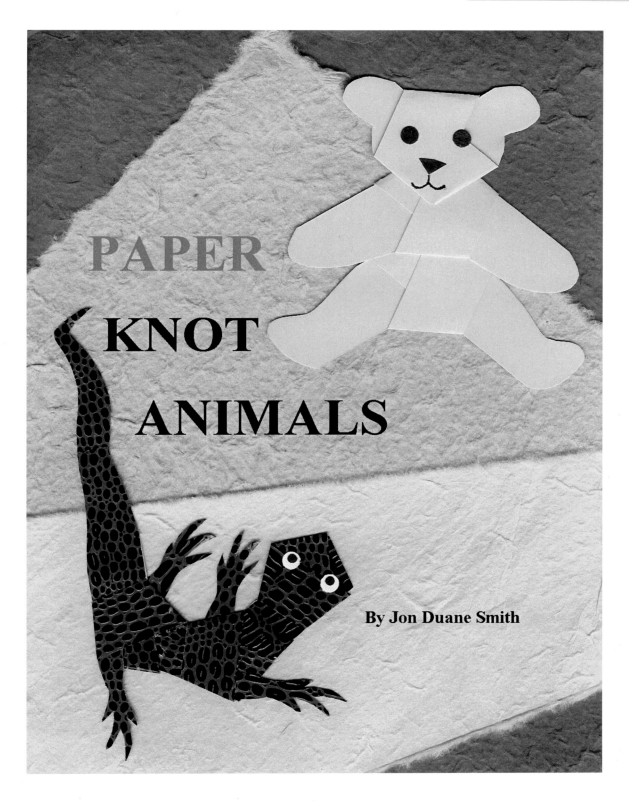

PAPER
KNOT
ANIMALS

By Jon Duane Smith

DEDICATED TO:

*My Family

*My students who always
  challenged me to do my best.

*My colleagues, friends, and
  teachers at Tippecanoe Valley
  School Corp.
      Akron, Mentone, and Burkett, IN

and thanks to:

*Leslie Kistler for computer editing

*Ann Allen for photo

*All the friends who encouraged

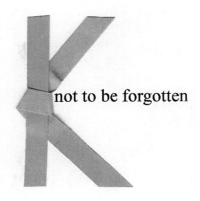not to be forgotten

3

An Introduction to Knot Animals

This paper art was inspired by a first grade class who found it difficult or impossible to tie a knot that would fasten a tail to a kite they had designed to catch the winds of March. As an art teacher in an act of desperation to teach kids how to tie a simple knot, a brown paper strip was picked up from the floor and experimentally used to tie a knot. Holding the paper knot at arm's length and with eyes squinted, the knot was turned this way then that way, when an imaginary bear's head appeared. Cutting around an ear on one end of the knot, then the other, magically the head of a bear emerged. Another strip was knotted and snipped to become the midsection and arms. A third paper strip was tied, trimmed, and assembled to create the complete figure of a bear. Wow! Gr-r-reat! The first knot animal was born. ('98)

Then the ever-wondering mind of an art teacher began to ask, "I wonder if a cat would work?" a bird, a dog, etc . . . . Many evenings were spent engaged in tying paper knots to construct a menagrie of paper animals. It worked

Students soon began tying paper knots to create their favorite animals. One student was heard to say, "This is easier than Origami!" With a little effort the students liked the quick effective results of tying paper knots to create expressive animal figures .

And you can easily make 2-D knot animals too. Let's try.

IT IS JUST

PAPER KNOTS !

It is American Origami and as simple as one, two, three paper knots.

We learn to :

1. Tie paper knots.

2. Cut Paper
    - use the cutaway scrap as a pattern
      to create a symmetrical figure.

3. Interlock knots to create a complete figure.

4. Add de tails (details)

    - ears   legs   stripes
    - eyes   tails   dots
    - nose   texture   etc.....

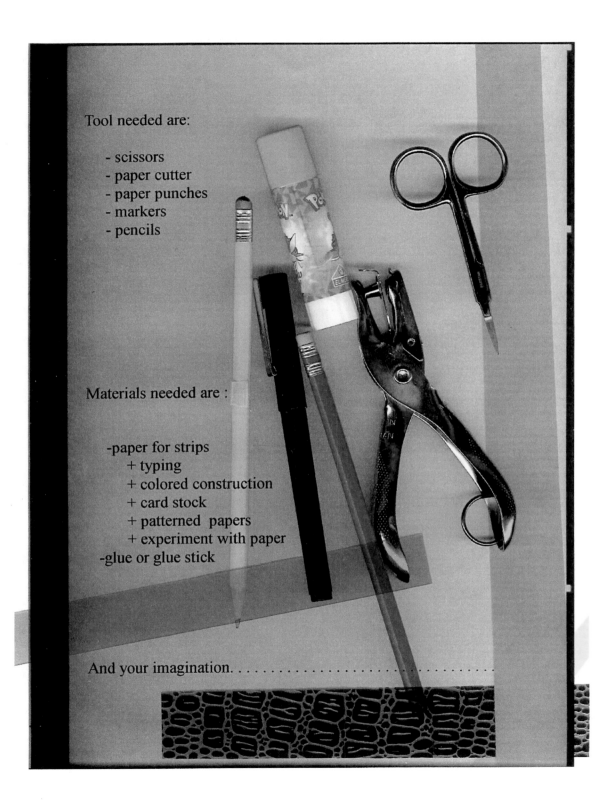

Tool needed are:

- scissors
- paper cutter
- paper punches
- markers
- pencils

Materials needed are :

-paper for strips
  + typing
  + colored construction
  + card stock
  + patterned papers
  + experiment with paper
-glue or glue stick

And your imagination. . . . .

WIDTH AND LENGTH
OF
PAPER STRIPS

The width of a strip will determine
the size of any figure.

1"   3/4"   1/2"

The lengths of paper can vary.
Two knots can be tied within a longer strip
of paper.

ADDING de TAILS

Adding the right details can charmingly enhance the character of a knot animal.

-Paper punches make good EYES.
  -Also stick-on pop out eyes are good or fold and cut your own styles.

-EARS can be as simple as basic triangles or as original as your own fold and cut designs.

- A NOSE can be drawn on with markers or made of glued on cut paper.

-LEGS and FEET can be as simple as sticks or be drawn more realistically, cut and glued.

-TAILS can be custom designed and attached with glue.

-TEXTURES can be applied with markers or pencils or select textured print paper to construct the figures.

INTERLOCKING PAPER KNOTS

Most animals figures can be constructed with three paper knots which require interlocking the knots to form the body.

To interlock-
Insert an end into each knot
hiding the ends and forming the body.

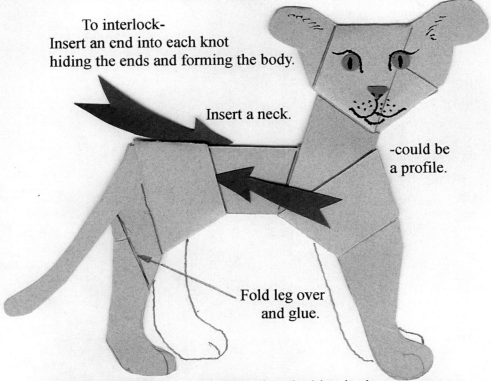

Insert a neck.

-could be
a profile.

Fold leg over
and glue.

* Add a third knot to the figure interlocking in the same manner and forming the head.
* Pose the figure in an expressive attitude or gesture then glue.
* Complete the character by adding details such as: eyes,
    -nose, mouth, tail, another set of legs, and neck if necessary.

POSING

By arranging the knots in thoughtful ways, a variety of postures with attitude can be achieved.

TO TIE A PAPER KNOT

The paper knot is the basic construction unit of any figure.

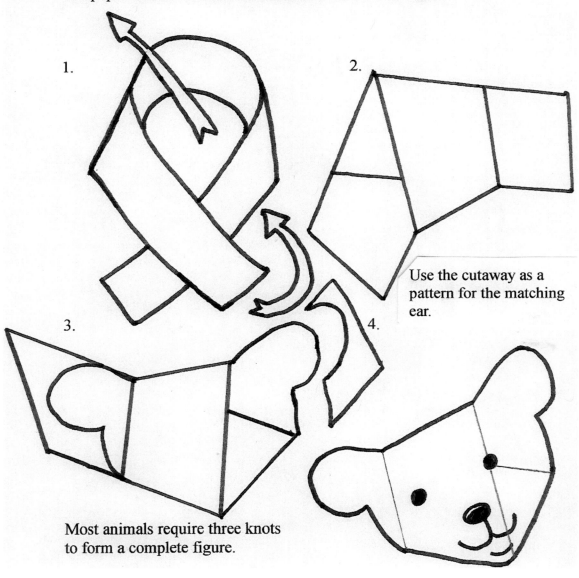

1.

2.

Use the cutaway as a pattern for the matching ear.

3.

4.

Most animals require three knots to form a complete figure.

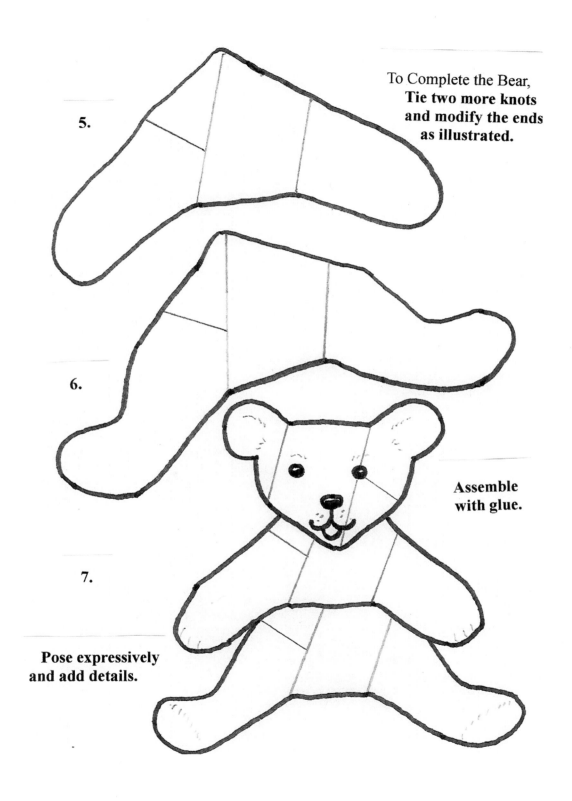

5.

To Complete the Bear,
**Tie two more knots
and modify the ends
as illustrated.**

6.

**Assemble
with glue.**

7.

**Pose expressively
and add details.**

Uses for Knot Animals

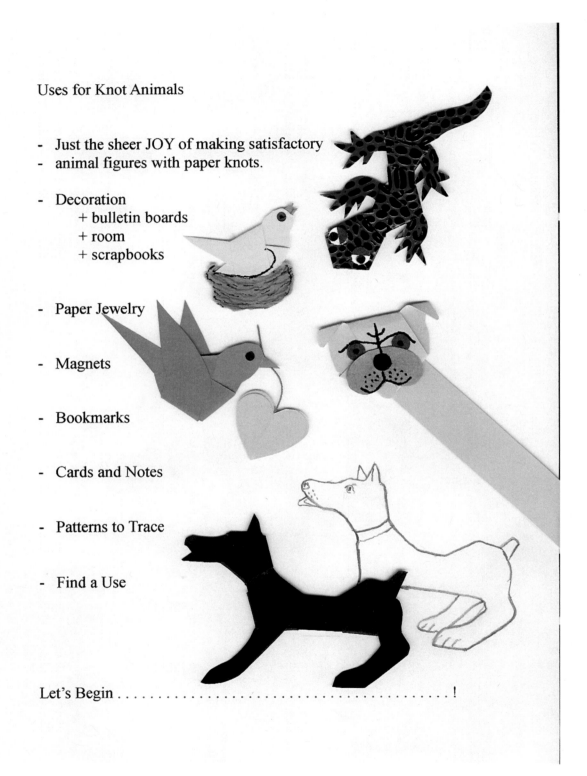

- Just the sheer JOY of making satisfactory
- animal figures with paper knots.

- Decoration
    + bulletin boards
    + room
    + scrapbooks

- Paper Jewelry

- Magnets

- Bookmarks

- Cards and Notes

- Patterns to Trace

- Find a Use

Let's Begin . . . . !

BOOKMARKS

Just a knot tied onto a paper strip can become a bookmark.

USE
KNOT ANIMALS
TO SEND A SPECIAL
NOTE.

ADAPT ANY FIGURE
TO CARRY A
MESSAGE.

PARTY FAVORS

ART ACTIVITIES

1. Make a collection of knot animals.

2. Make a knot animal and create an environment using a choice of medium.

3. Make a composition of knot animals.

4. Make knot animals to illustrate a story.

If you can make a BEAR,
    you can make all other animals.
        It is as simple as one, two, three paper knots.

What animal do you want to make?   _____?_____

Choose your strips of an appropriate color.

Make three paper knots.

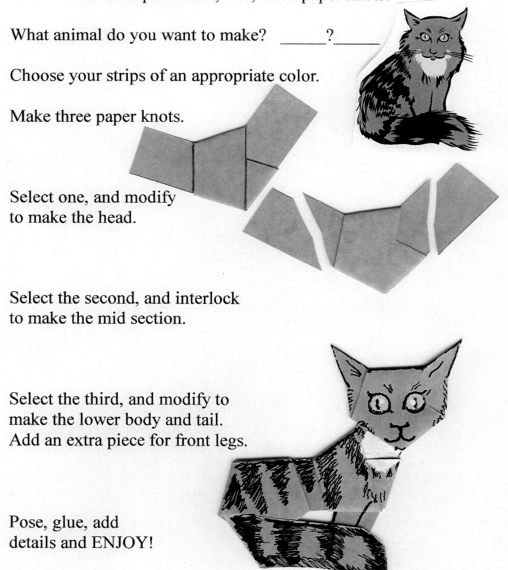

Select one, and modify
to make the head.

Select the second, and interlock
to make the mid section.

Select the third, and modify to
make the lower body and tail.
Add an extra piece for front legs.

Pose, glue, add
details and ENJOY!

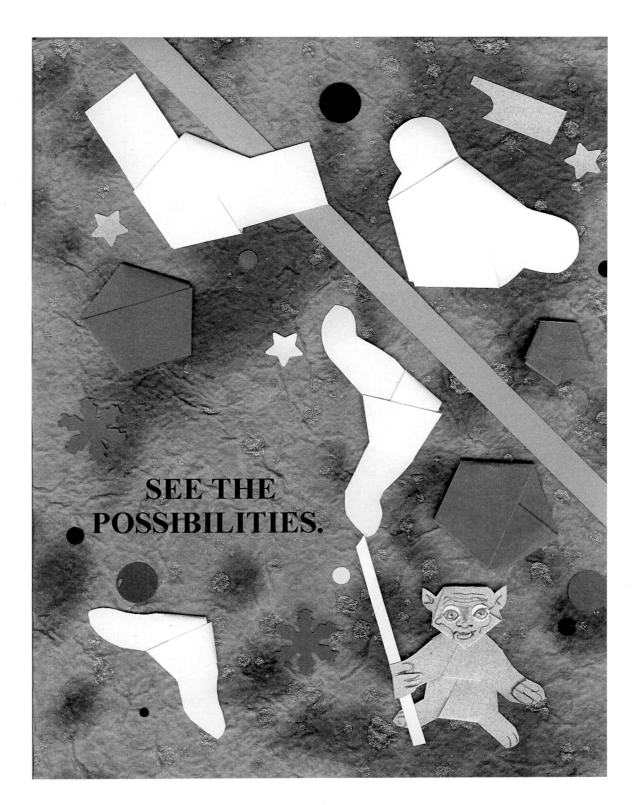

SEE THE
POSSIBILITIES.

BEARS

and more BEARS

CATS

DOGS

BIRDS

FARM ANIMALS

ALL KINDS OF ANIMALS CAN BE MADE WITH PAPER KNOTS.

SOMETIMES TWO

NOTS
WILL DO.

SOMETIMES ONE

NOT WILL DO.

DESIGNER LIZARDS

IT IS EASY AS 1, 2, & 3

1. Select a subject.
2. Tie the appropriate knots.
3. Assemble and detail.

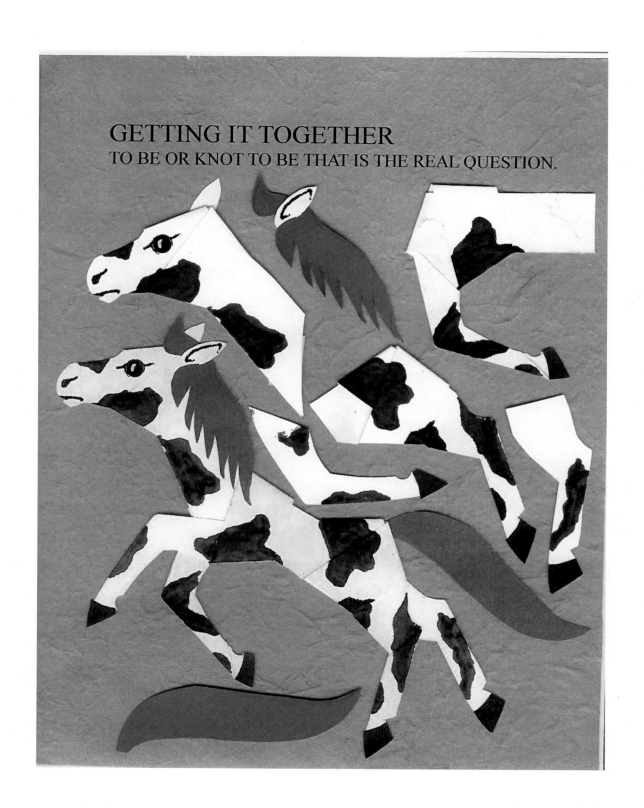

ABOUT THE AUTHOR

Jon Duane Smith was born February 3, 1942 in South Bend, Indiana and was country-raised near Akron, Indiana where he graduated from high school in 1960. After attending Manchester College, he returned to his high school to for a total of thirty-five years teaching various grade levels of elementary, junior high, and high school art. One interim year, 1969-70 he taught at Manchester High School, North Manchester, Indiana for a teaching career of thirty-six years. In 1973, he received a Masters Degree in Art Education from Saint Francis College, Fort Wayne, Indiana. Smith retired from active teaching in May 2001.

Printed in Victoria, Canada

Note for Librarians: a cataloguing record for this book that includes Dewey Classification and US Library of Congress numbers is available from the National Library of Canada. The complete cataloguing record can be obtained from the National Library's online database at: www.nlc-bnc.ca/amicus/index-e.html

ISBN 1-4120-1379-8

TRAFFORD

This book was published on-demand in cooperation with Trafford Publishing.
On-demand publishing is a unique process and service of making a book available for retail sale to the public taking advantage of on-demand manufacturing and Internet marketing. On-demand publishing includes promotions, retail sales, manufacturing, order fulfilment, accounting and collecting royalties on behalf of the author.

Suite 6E, 2333 Government St., Victoria, B.C. V8T 4P4, CANADA

Phone 250-383-6864   Toll-free   1-888-232-4444 (Canada & US)
Fax   250-383-6804   E-mail sales@trafford.com
Web site www.trafford.com   TRAFFORD PUBLISHING IS A DIVISION OF TRAFFORD HOLDINGS LTD.
Trafford Catalogue #03-1757   www.trafford.com/robots/03-1757.html

10   9   8   7   6   5   4   3   2